DATE DUE

JUL 2 7 2007	
10-1-15	
10-16-15	

THE MONSTER FROM UNDERGROUND

Crabtree Publishing Company
www.crabtreebooks.com

PMB 16A, 350 Fifth Avenue
Suite 3308
New York, NY 10118

612 Welland Avenue
St. Catharines, Ontario
Canada, L2M 5V6

Cross, Gillian.
    The monster from underground / Gillian Cross ; illustrated by Chris
Priestley.
      p. cm. -- (Yellow bananas)
    Summary: Buddy hates to write and is unhappy about having to keep a nature
diary for a week until he decides to survey the night sky and discovers something
weird in his neighbor's backyard that makes for a truly interesting diary.
      ISBN 0-7787-0935-3 (RHC) -- ISBN 0-7787-0981-7 (pbk.)
      [1. Diaries--Fiction. 2. Dinosaurs--Fiction. 3. Schools--Fiction.] I. Priestley,
Chris, ill. II. Title. III. Series.
PZ7.C88253 Mo 2003
[Fic]--dc21
                      2002009607
                      LC

Published by Crabtree Publishing in 2002
Published in 2000 by Egmont Children's Books Limited
Text copyright © Gillian Cross 1990
Illustrations copyright © Chris Priestley 2000
The Author and Illustrator have asserted their moral rights.
Reinforced Hardcover Binding ISBN 0-7787-0935-3 Paperback ISBN 0-7787-0981-7

1 2 3 4 5 6 7 8 9 0 Printed in Italy 0 9 8 7 6 5 4 3 2

THE MONSTER FROM UNDERGROUND

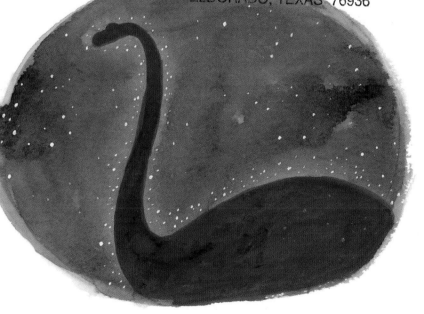

GILLIAN CROSS
Illustrated by Chris Priestley

YELLOW BANANAS

To Anthony
G.C.

For Glenn
C.P.

Chapter One

BUDDY WILSON WAS brilliant. He was great at soccer, a star at snooker, and a genius at video games. He knew about computers, airplanes, and dinosaurs and he had the best bicycle in the whole school.

But he HATED writing.

Whenever Mrs. Evans, his teacher, said, "Get out your pens," Buddy shuddered. He could never write more than a few words, about anything. After that, his hand ached from holding the pen, and his brain ached even more.

So he was horrified when Mrs. Evans told them about the Nature Diary

"First," she said, "choose something to watch for a week. Write a little bit about it every day – just before you go to bed."

For a week! Buddy shuddered.

"Can we watch anything we like?" asked Kevin.

Harriet Newton tossed her head. "*I'm* going to make a rain gauge to put in my backyard. Then I can write about the weather every day. How much rain there's been and –"

"I'll watch my dog," Paul said, interrupting. They all interrupted Harriet, because she never stopped talking. "I'll notice what he does every day."

Mrs. Evans beamed. "That's the idea. Watch for seven days – and keep an open mind. Then at the end of the week, write down what you have learned. There will be a prize for the best one."

Seven days of writing! At home! Buddy sat and frowned as everyone chatted about their diaries. By the end of the day, he was the only person in the class who did not have an idea.

"Look for something interesting on your way home," Mrs. Evans said.

So he looked hard. What he saw was the road construction.

They were cutting through Hawthorn Hill, for the new highway, and all the different layers of

rock were showing. Just like layers in a slice of cake, except that each layer of rock was older than the one above.

Buddy stared at them. Those rocks had been hidden under the ground for millions and millions of years and suddenly there they were, up on top again. Now that *was* interesting.

And perhaps he could write about it in his Nature Diary! He grinned and got his book out, to make a sketch.

But Harriet was right behind him, and she hooted with laughter. "Hey, everyone! Buddy is going to write a Nature Diary about *road construction!*"

"It's the rocks not the road construction," said Buddy.

But Harriet didn't listen. She just laughed louder. "Watch those diggers, Buddy! Perhaps one of them will have a sweet little baby digger! Or spin a web and catch an airplane!"

"Shut up!" said Buddy.

But Harriet went on about vegetarian tractors and wild, meat-eating diggers, all the way home. And it *was* all the way, because she lived next door to Buddy.

So he didn't have a moment to think about his Nature Diary.

Chapter Two

THE NEXT DAY was Tuesday, and Mrs. Evans kept nagging him about choosing something for the diary. But he couldn't think of a thing.

To make it worse, Harriet spent all day teasing him about diggers. She even kept it up while they walked home, which made him rush past the road construction without stopping.

And that was too bad, because the machines had opened up a whole new layer since the day before. The new layer was made up of a different kind of rock, with strange, interesting-looking lumps in it. But Buddy didn't look closely, because of Harriet.

When he got home – there was Harriet's mother, drinking coffee and going on about the rain gauge.

Buddy's mother frowned as he came in. "What are *you* doing for this Nature Diary, Bernard?"

"I'm still deciding." Buddy shuffled his feet.

Mrs. Newton rattled on without taking any notice, just like Harriet.

" . . . and she checks that gauge every five minutes, to see how much rain she's collected. I had to *make* her go to bed last night."

That was when Buddy had an idea. If Mrs. Newton *made* Harriet go to bed at night – he would do his Nature Diary then! He could sneak out every night, at midnight, and do a survey of the night sky! If he did it at night, he wouldn't have to put up with Harriet laughing at him over the fence.

It was brilliant! He didn't tell his mother, of course, but he immediately set the alarm on his watch.

It woke him up just before midnight, beeping quietly in his ear. By five to twelve he was standing in the backyard, looking up at the sky.

Half the sky. The other half was hidden by the Newtons' apple tree. He needed to climb higher to get a better view. Standing on the compost pile, he scrambled on to the shed roof and took a good look around.

That was when he saw them.

There were three round gray things, lying in
a patch of moonlight in the middle of Harriet's
lawn. They were as big as footballs, but not
quite ball-shaped. More like eggs.

Eggs? How could they be? What animal laid
eggs the size of footballs?

All the lights were off in the Newtons' house.
Quietly, Buddy slid down into their garden and
walked across the lawn, to have a better look at
the strange gray objects.

They were definitely eggs. Huge, *enormous* eggs. He put out his hand to feel the shells, but just before he touched them he noticed something else. Something that made him snatch his hand back, as fast as he could.

Footprints.

There were two of them. They were at least as long as his skateboard, and deep too, as if they'd been made by something very heavy.

Between them was a long, deep groove, like the mark of a dragging tail.

Except that this tail had to be the size of a tree trunk.

Buddy stared. It was frightening, standing next to those giant eggs and looking at those enormous footprints – but it was a great chance to begin his Nature Diary. He began to sketch the eggs and the footprints, as fast as he could.

Then a voice hissed behind him. "What are you doing?"

He turned around and saw Harriet, glaring at him.

"Have you been fiddling with my rain gauge?" she snapped.

"Your rain gauge?" Buddy almost laughed. "Who cares about that? Just look at these amazing eggs. And the footprints."

"Eggs?" Harriet said. "Footprints? What are you talking about?"

"You must be blind! Can't you see –" Buddy whirled around, to point at them – and stopped dead.

There was only the empty lawn. The eggs and the footprints had vanished.

Chapter Three

THE NEXT DAY, Harriet's father came by as soon as he got home from work. To complain.

"Bernard's been tampering with Harriet's rain gauge."

It was no use arguing. Buddy's mother wouldn't listen. She lost her temper and sent him straight to bed.

Buddy made a face, but he really was tired. He laid down on the bed to read a comic book and fell asleep immediately, without undressing or closing the curtains.

When his alarm went off at quarter to twelve, he woke up and blinked. For a moment he couldn't think what was going on, because he had forgotten all about the survey of the night sky. And then, suddenly, he was wide awake.

Something had moved, just outside the window.

There was no shape to be seen. Just darkness. But the darkness had rippled and *moved*.

For a few seconds, Buddy was too frightened to breathe. Then the rippling happened again.

Very slowly, as if something was crawling past the window. On and on and on.

But it was an *upstairs* window! What was big enough to block that? It would have to be bigger than an elephant!

Whatever it was, it wasn't looking in. Quietly he crawled out of bed and crept over to the window. Pressing his nose to the glass, he peered out at the large moving blob. It was rough and wrinkled, a bit like an elephant's skin.

And where the moonlight caught it, he
could see blotches and streaks.

Buddy's heart thudded with fright, but he
wouldn't let himself run back to bed. Whatever the
creature was, it was much too big to get into the
room. It was worth trying to get a better look at it.

Carefully, Buddy unlatched the window. It
squeaked a bit, but whatever was outside didn't
take any notice. The skin just went on rippling
past as he pushed the window open.

The smell nearly
knocked him over.

It was like old grass
cuttings and rotting
plants, mixed with
mushrooms and stale
cabbage.

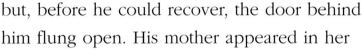

Buddy clapped
his hand over his nose
but, before he could recover, the door behind
him flung open. His mother appeared in her

bathrobe, looking
angry.

"Bernard, what
are you doing? You
woke me up from
a deep sleep!"

Didn't she notice
the smell? Buddy
waved at the
window. "Look!"

"At what?" said
his mother.

Buddy turned back to the window, but the smell was gone. No rough, blotchy skin. Just the dark sky, with the moon shining through the Newtons' apple tree.

The giant whatever-it-was had vanished.

His mother made him go right back to bed, but the moment she was out of the way, he switched on his nightstand light. Very strange things were happening, and he wanted to make sure he remembered them. Grabbing his Nature Diary, he started to write.

I have just seen something very peculiar outside my window . . .

Chapter Four

ON THURSDAY, Buddy made a plan. He knew it was no use trying to tell people about the eggs and the wrinkled skin and the giant footprints. No one would believe a word of it.

He needed a witness.

Next time something strange happened, there had to be someone else there. Not one of his friends. Someone who wouldn't back him up unless he was telling the truth.

And he knew the ideal person.

At twenty minutes to twelve that night, he was standing in the Newtons' backyard, throwing little stones up at Harriet's window to wake her up.

It worked like a charm because the window was open. Harriet stuck her head out, looking furious.

"*Buddy?* What's going on? That hit me on the nose."

"Shhh!" Buddy said.

"Come down."

"Why? If you've touched my rain gauge –"

Buddy didn't bother to answer. He just backed away from the window and waited, staring up at the big, bright moon behind the apple tree. After a few minutes, Harriet crept through the backdoor.

"Are you crazy?" she hissed. "My dad will go berserk if he catches you in our backyard again. What do you want?"

"Wait a bit, and I'll show you," muttered Buddy. "And be quiet."

They waited. They stood with their backs to the house, staring down the hill. Far below, they could see the road construction but even that was still and quiet.

"It's funny," Harriet whispered. "Everything's very bright, but there's no moon."

"Yes there is," said Buddy. "Up behind the apple tree. It –"

And then he stopped. Harriet was right. There wasn't a moon behind the apple tree, and there weren't any stars either. Instead, there was a big, black patch, as if something was standing between them and the sky. Something very big.

"Harriet –"

But before he could warn her, the black shape moved and they saw it clearly. The monster. It had a massive, humped body and a long, thick neck that reached into the sky. Its head looked ridiculously small as it peered over the top of the house.

Harriet gasped. She clutched at Buddy's arm and he clutched hers.

Slowly, the small head swayed from side to side, and they caught a whiff of the mushroomy, rotten-grass smell.

Then Harriet gulped. "Look at the apple tree!"

The creature's head bent down to grab at the top of the tree and the leaves shook, furiously.

When the head reared up again, there were black, leafy shapes sticking out of its mouth. A slow crunching sound came from somewhere up in the sky.

Buddy didn't dare to move, but he stared at the little head and the long, long neck. They reminded him of something. If only he could remember what . . .

And then – it vanished.

Suddenly, there was nothing there, except the big, white moon, behind the black branches of the apple tree. Harriet took a deep breath.

"What *was* it?"

"I don't know," said Buddy. "But I'm certainly going to find out."

When he got back to his bedroom, he wrote down all the details, underneath what he had written the day before.

. . . its body must have been as tall as our house and its neck reached even higher. It was a very long, thin neck, with a small head . . .

He lay awake for hours, trying to think where he had seen a neck and a head like that before. But his brain refused to work. He fell asleep at half past four, without having remembered.

But when he woke up the next morning, he *knew*.

He jumped out of bed and rummaged through the bottom of his closet. There were a bunch of plastic tubs in there, full of old toys and games. Building blocks. Plastic airplanes. Model soldiers with their trucks and weapons. And somewhere . . .

The tub he was looking for was right at the bottom. He tugged it out and emptied it on to the floor.

There were dozens of little plastic dinosaurs, all different shapes and colors. He shuffled through them, tossing away the stegosaurus and the tyrannosaurus, the parasaurolophus and the iguanadon.

Suddenly, he found the one he was looking for. He gazed at the long neck and the little head for a moment, and then turned it over to read the name underneath, to make sure he was right.

DIPLODOCUS.

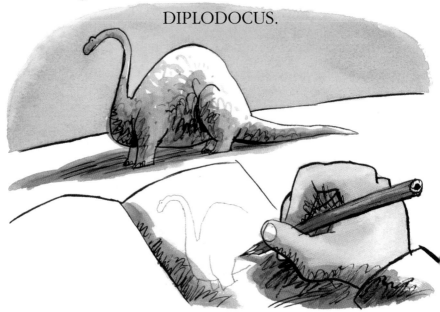

Standing it on his night table, he sketched the shape carefully in his Nature Diary. Then he pushed it into his pocket. All the way to school, his fingers were curled around the thick body, feeling the long, long neck and the long, long tail.

Was it *possible*?

behind them. And then, slowly – very slowly –
the giant black shape of the diplodocus began
to move.

Buddy shivered. Suppose the monster saw
them? Suppose it knocked the shed over?
Suppose –

But it was no good thinking about that. If
they wanted photographs, they had to stay there.
He forced himself to hold the camera steady.

"Now!" hissed Harriet.

Both cameras flashed at once. The light was
like an explosion, much brighter than Buddy
had expected. It must have surprised the
diplodocus too. Slowly, but not quite as slowly
as before, it moved again – towards them.

Its head reared up, on top of its long neck,
and began to sway from side to side, searching.
Getting closer and closer. Harriet gulped.

"Let's get out of here!"

Buddy shook his head. "Wait. I don't think
it'll hurt us. It's supposed to be a vegetarian."
Crossing his fingers hard, he hoped all those
scientists were right.

The head swayed closer and closer. It was small for such a huge animal – but it looked enormous as it came toward them. Lower and lower it bent, until Buddy and Harriet were looking straight into its eyes.

The eyes of a dinosaur.

The eyes were very pale, like pools of rainwater, and empty. Buddy stared deep into them. He couldn't tell whether the diplodocus saw them, but he was too scared to move.

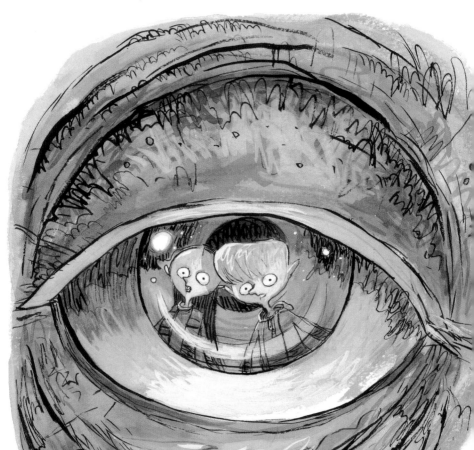

Then Harriet grabbed his arm. "Photos!" she whispered. "We'll never get another chance like this."

Together, they lifted their cameras. Buddy got the focus right and made sure the dinosaur's head was in the center of his viewfinder. Then he said, "Now!"

And the flashes went off together.

What happened next was mind-boggling.

Buddy wrote it all down in his Nature Diary the next morning.

. . . when the lights flashed, the dinosaur began to move toward us again. We couldn't escape, because it was too close. For one second, we could see it lurching forward and then everything went dark and very strange. Tingling.

The diplodocus walked right through us.

Chapter Six

HARRIET GOT THE photos developed on Saturday
morning, and she took them right to Buddy's
house. When he opened the door, he could see
that she was upset.

"What's the matter, Harry?"

"It's these. Look." She held out the photographs.

There were four beautiful pictures of the full
moon behind the apple tree – but no sign of a
dinosaur in any of them.

"There's nothing there," said Harriet. "Did we
imagine it?"

Buddy shook his head. "I don't think so.
Come down to the road construction. I want to
show you something."

They walked down together to the construction site in Hawthorn Hill and stared at the layers of rock. Like layers in a slice of cake – except that each layer was older than the one above.

"The bottom layer must be very old indeed," Harriet said slowly.

Buddy nodded. "About a hundred and fifty million years."

"And those strange, enormous lumps?"

"Bones," said Buddy. "I guess."

Harriet frowned. "Someone ought to have a look at them."

"I've been thinking about that," said Buddy. "I think I'll write to the local paper."

"Write? *You?*"

Harriet howled with laughter, but Buddy just grinned.

Chapter Seven

TWO WEEKS LATER, Buddy finished his Nature
Diary. On the first page he glued his best
newspaper clippings. There was a large
photograph of his face and underneath it said:

Bernard °Buddy' Wilson

Diplodocus

SCHOOLBOY'S DINOSAUR FIND

Schoolboy Bernard Wilson (above left) has
sharp eyes! He noticed some strange lumps
in the excavation for the new M39 and wrote
to his local paper about them. Now scientists
believe that the lumps are fossilized bones of a
diplodocus (above right) — a huge dinosaur that
has been extinct for millions of years.

There was a sketch of the diplodocus, too. The artist had got the face a bit wrong and drawn the skin all scaly, but it was definitely the creature they had seen in Harriet's backyard. After he glued the newspaper clipping in, Buddy read through the whole diary again. He was amazed to see how much he had written. There was only one page left, and he knew what had to go on that. Picking up his pen, he began to write.

WHAT I'VE LEARNED

I'm sure we saw a diplodocus. Not a real one, because someone else would have noticed that. And a live diplodocus couldn't have walked through us.

I think it was a ghost. It started walking when its bones came to the surface in the road construction. And it's stopped now that the bones have been discovered.

I've thought a lot about this, Mrs. Evans. Keeping an open mind, like you said. And I can't see any other explanation.

Mrs. Evans was delighted with Buddy's diary.

Well done! she wrote. *It's a crazy idea but it makes a good story. At last you've managed to write a lot!*

She gave him two gold stars and a special prize for the Most Original Entry.

Mrs. Evans didn't say she believed Buddy's story, but she kept the newspaper article. She also promised the class a trip to see the dinosaur.

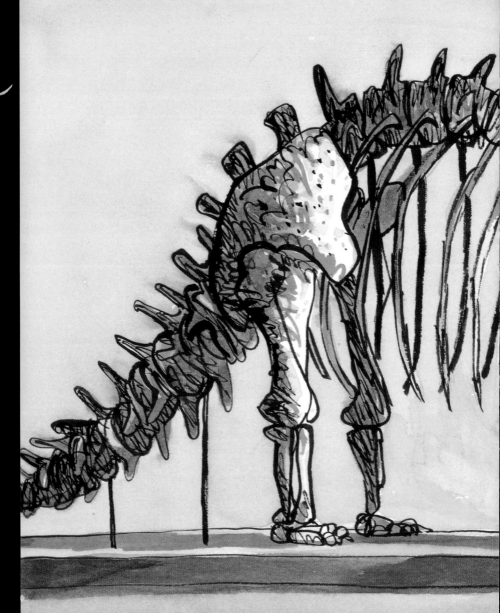

Diplodocus

 **YELLOW BANANAS**

Don't forget there's a whole bunch of Yellow Bananas to choose from:

Amina's Blanket
A Break in the Chain
Colly's Barn
Dragon Trouble
Fine Feathered Friend
Jo-Jo the Melon Donkey
The Monster from Underground
My Brother Bernadette
Soccer Star
Storm
Stranger from Somewhere in Time
Who's a Clever Girl?